THE BELLE OF THE BALL

LINDSAY BARRETT

Act 1

Scene: A large bedroom with adjoining dining room, study, bathroom and toilet, upstairs in a large, sixteen room house overlooking three gardens and a church, atop a Cornish fishing village with a view to the sea. A naked man and woman are laid on top of a large double bed with a window open looking out onto the sea. It is morning time with a clear view of the church.

Jane: You have totally corrupted me. Before I met with you I was pure of spirit and soul. Now I am completely corrupted by anal sex...What is it that people will call us?...Well, you know all the right words.

Alex: Sodomites.

Jane: No, better than that.

Alex: Catamites?

Jane: Yes, that is what we are. Heaving, sweating catamites in our debased little nest.

Alex: Your problem is that you act so fucking superior. So self-contained in your ladylike manner, peering out at the rest of us from within your ivory tower...Pure of soul and spirit you say. Why, when we first met you already had two children and you promptly told me I was the first person you'd ever had a proper orgasm with. If you can believe that. Christ, the blessed virgin, how is that possible?...Alright, alright, I know I may have an A-level in Biology, but I am not a specialist in human biology...This small, debased little nest, you say. More like sixteen rooms of Cornish gloom, if you ask me...No, don't go pulling a face like that, it makes you look dead plug ugly. If you don't like anal sex so much how come you keep enticing me with you swaying, wriggling arse!

Jane: Oh, please, stop it. You don't really mean it. I am not complaining. It's just, well, I never fully imagined when I was a bright young sixteen year old girl of promise and ambition that I would find myself nineteen years later howling at the moon and excited at the idea of toilet sex. You never quite know what is waiting around the corner for you, do you!

Alex: So true.

Jane: Sarcasm is the lowest form of wit.

Alex: Don't these seagulls ever give up their ceaseless screeching. Christ, that damn noise. The same hoarse croaking and screeching on demand by the hour. It never stops here!

Jane: What do you expect. We are by the sea...Auntie and Mum could never have imagined what was going to happen to them...

Alex: Would it have changed anything if they had known...I doubt it...What is that book by a Russian author whereby the main character is about to commit suicide and gets stopped and given a second chance by a magician to relive his life afresh and gradually forgets that he is getting a second chance and goes and commits the self-same follies and mistakes all over again right on cue...

Jane: I just cannot remember anything anymore. Anal sex does that to me. It is so utterly strange and weird. As if I am floating outside of humanity all of the time. Body on fire, brain all frozen. All the while I am fighting to hold you off. I can sense your basic intentions. You are trying hard to raise the Babylonian whore out of me and I will not let her through. Draw out the archetype for some diversionary game that you have devised. More material for yet another bloody novel that nobody is really interested in.

Alex: What time do we set off then?

Jane: Not very subtle at changing the subject, are we?

Alex: It hurts.

Jane: How do you begin to deal with it then?

Alex: When I lived in that Watchtower on to the way to Penzance, one night, do you remember, you found that new writing magazine for me? You see, it's not just your arse I'm addicted to. I'm addicted to your brain as well.

Jane: Aren't I the lucky one then!

Alex: Well, the New Writing people wrote back to me after my first submission and accepted three of my short stories for publication...

Jane: This was shortly after you walked out on me and publicly declared you never ever wanted to see me again!

Alex: Well, it's very hard to be rational and caring at the self-same time when your fiendish lover is clinging onto your ankles in the middle of a Cornish street and yelling at the top of her lungs 'You can't leave me! You can't leave me! Please don't go!'...All the lace net curtains in the street were a-twitching with the furtive activity.

Jane: You kicked me!

Alex: Yes, I did and you pleaded for more...To continue, I had just got back to the Watchtower from selling a video cover in Bude. Sat cross-legged on the floor of my Watchtower room and rolling a giant-sized spliff. Short stories for publication and also having them included in an anthology put out by the magazine at the end of the year. What did I discover? That the New Writing magazine had just gone bust and folded after only six issues and all I had to show was an apologetic letter...You can laugh!

Jane: I laughed when you kicked me in the street!

Alex: No, that wasn't a laugh. That was a howl of desperate rage and sorrow...Rejection is hard to take. How many people can take a meaningful 'No'. I learnt that lesson as a space salesman. It never gets any easier. Most people can't suffer the simplest rejection...Rejection...Rejection...Can't stomach repeated no's, you see...I smoked that giant spliff after the drive back from Bude in the Cornish rain and imagined all artists, writers and poets to be like sperm heads. A fit, active, sexually healthy male may produce three million sperm heads at the point of ejaculation. Only one of those three million sperm warriors...

Jane: Sperm warriors!

Alex: Shush!

Jane: Don't you shush me, Alex Croy!

Alex: I love you. Now will you listen and pay attention.

Jane: If you say 'I love you' then that must cover all manner of interruptions. I wait, beg, need and plead for you to say it and you choose to slip it out in a moment like this! What am I supposed to do? Say I thank you and pray for small mercies!

Alex: Stop moving your body like that. It's so easy to get distracted when you're a practising catamite.

Jane: Very funny...Now go on if you must.

Alex: Even the screeching seagulls can't take their beady, fair-weather eyes off your arse...Only one sperm head can make it through. All the other two million, nine hundred and ninety-nine must die in the sexual act. Yet the triumphant one that makes it through could not get the chance to fertilise the female egg without the efforts of all the others. For every successful artist, writer and poet, there are thousands upon thousands of others

Jane:	beavering away. Dying, failing, disillusioned and finally abandoned. Unable to take any more no's. Maybe the coming ghost people just before the next gigantic flood hits, who knows.
Jane:	Did that thought truly console you? Make the rejection any easier to take?
Alex:	No, not really. But at least I toked on that giant spliff and felt like a sperm warrior carrying the load. Kaput. Bang. Shot to death. Here's to the next time.
Jane:	That is very funny. You don't know just how funny that is. All of your sperm heads end up martyred and dead, littering my anal passage. What are they trying to fertilise?...No! Please don't answer that question. Change the subject quick. Say the word bottom very slowly...Go on, say it, then I will give you the outlined itinerary for today...Please say it. I love it when you speak it slowly.
Alex:	Bottom.
Jane:	And again.
Alex:	Bottom...bottom...and you being an angelic, pure and debased sodomite and all.
Jane:	I much prefer catamite...I am not saying that it's not all my own fault. It's just that you have taken all my love for you and have used it to corrupt me with...Is that not true?...You cannot bring yourself to speak the words and just nod in case all these screeching seagulls record your admission...We leave at ten o'clock with Mum. I have asked Ben to come with us. He is so serene and angelic. He will soothe her worries, ease her nerves if she has any left. Susan is down with her at present and I have told her to have Mum ready on time.

(The church bells have started ringing. A dog within the house is barking ferociously.)

Alex:	This noise is driving me crazy!
Jane:	What?
Alex:	This noise...Oh, what the hell, I'm getting dressed. C'mon, Trini is crack-brained and neurotic. I told you so when you first got her. Absolutely nuts. Bad cross-breeding, weak in the head.

(Jane and Alex are getting dressed.)

Jane:	I just love the sound of those church bells. After the first few peals they make me start to cry…You see, Trini has stopped barking, Susan has quietened her down.
Alex:	Raw meat, I shouldn't wonder…Why do those church bells make you cry? Hurry, get dressed, we are running out of time.
Jane:	Because I feel I can never go home again. It is as if my relationship with the church, with God, has been severed since I've met up with you.
Alex:	You're blaming me now for losing your religion. Next thing it'll be Hiroshima, the Titanic, the Great Plague!
Jane:	Anal sex and that was you!
Alex:	Anal sex keeps popping up its' pretty little head in our conversation today.
Jane:	That is a strange way of putting it…I feel outside of God. I no longer feel **innate** goodness the way I once did when I was a child. If I see myself in a church with you, I just know that you will strip me naked, throw me face down over the altar and bugger me senseless.
Alex:	And you would thoroughly enjoy that.
Jane:	Exactly. That is why I am so cut off from God.
Alex:	But that is just your sexual fantasy. That is only an image playing around inside your head.
Jane:	Don't you see! That is what you have done to me. Not only have you corrupted me physically, but you have also done it mentally, spiritually and morally. I no longer care about anything else but you. That is so very wrong. I am lost, all at sea.
Alex:	The sea looks very calm out there today…Try being kind to yourself. We can't all remain innocent children for the rest of our days. We have to grow up. Accept responsibilities. Feed our carnal desires, satisfy our sexual cravings so that we don't become suppressed freaks who explode one day and kill the kids, sell the nation's secrets, contaminate the drinking water in this local Cornish fishing village of ours.
Jane:	Yes, but I no longer know who I am.
Alex:	So!

Jane: Well, what really worries me is that I don't care when I'm with you.

Alex: Look on the bright side, at least you know your name, know where you are and can remember things from one minute to the next. You could be Dorothy. Lost in a blank universe. Clutching at movements and not really knowing life at all.

Jane: But she does have her moments…I feel better now those church bells have stopped ringing. They were trying to call me back to God, but I don't want to go. I just want you inside of me all of the time, body and soul. I am utterly shameless.

Alex: You are and I love you for it.

Jane: You only say that to encourage me, lead me further on…You know when we had to send Auntie away, well, Mum had one of her last lucid moments. I was helping her to get dressed so we could travel to the Home with Auntie…

Alex: You've already told me this about a dozen times.

Jane: You are so very unkind. Let me tell you once again. Don't you realise that people have a need to continually repeat incidents. It can help you the better to understand what is happening in your life. Like broken pieces of a jigsaw puzzle that wash up on the seashore and you suddenly have the shocking realisation that they represent broken pieces of your own soggy life!

Alex: All right, Jane dear, what did your mother, Dorothy, say to you as you helped her get dressed in the summer sun?

Jane: You are such an arsehole, you know, and anyway it was wintertime as you well know…She suddenly looked right up at me and said 'I feel like I have been lifted up and put down into someone else's life'…Isn't that sad!

Alex: What did you say back to her?

Jane: I didn't know rightly what to say. We were never really touchy, feely people like you. If that had been your mother you would have put your arm around her shoulder and have made physical contact…I just felt stunned. Like I was permanently about to lose my mother though she was alive. Auntie gone as well. And now today I feel like I have lost myself. I feel stranded…Do you know what is even worse than me not being able to believe?

Alex: No, what is worse?

(Jane throws a pillow in mock anger at Alex's head which misses.)

Jane: I put you before my children. My two boys suffer because of my relationship with you. That cannot be right. I never thought I could ever do such a thing.

Alex: Are you enjoying yourself? Do you feel excited each day, alive to the heat and the jive?

Jane: Yes...But not today. I will feel better when today is all over. It is so awfully sad to me. I mean, why her!

Alex: Look, it is a long shot, but you never know, something may just trigger her to remember. All the doctors, psychiatrists, trick cyclists and so-called medical experts in the whole wide world don't really know. Certainly up until a few years ago most experts under the sun called it the onset of old age, senility, dementia. Batty old granny still living with her family and dribbling into her food with a faraway look in her eyes...No, more like a totally blank look in her eyes. Now we are all experts today and can give a name to Alzheimer's disease if we can remember it...Sorry, just can't resist. You've got to laugh ass the saucy French actress said to the Nazi priest. Jackboots and a dog collar make strange bed companions.

Jane: Stop it! You think you are being really witty, but you are just cruel and unfunny!

Alex: You smiled.

Jane: Well, I must be a complete idiot then.

Alex: What I mean to say is that the good Doctor Alzheimer did not lend his name to the condition until sometime in the late eighteen hundreds...All right, I know full well that we all have a better chance of contracting the condition, but it must have always been with us. Back in the times of Ancient Greece there must have been lots of people who lived to age seventy-five. They never smoked cigarettes, mainlined heroin, freebased coke, drank five bottles of vodka a day or ate highly processed foods. But, of course, all of this has been forgotten in the endless march of progress and, for your information, Miss Godless Sister, anal intercourse between men and women was considered very good back in Ancient Greece because it was and remains the best form of contraception. Not called the Italian method for nothing, dear.

Jane: Pope Paul will be pleased!

Alex: He will, bless you, my child, but stark naked out in the woods for sure. You can never trust those Polish fuckers.

Jane: Don't curse so much, it doesn't suit you. We had better go downstairs and help Susan. Do we take Trini with us?

Alex: I don't think she is safe to take on a long journey. Like as not we will not be back until after dark. Does Dorothy really want bloody Trini sandwiched in between her and angelic Ben, scratching on the backseat and barking all the way to Salcombe and back? I think not. You will get upset. The dog will panic and be sick because she will think she is doing wrong and letting yummy mummy, you, down. As I said, weak in the head.

Jane: You just cannot wait to get onto your pet subject, genetics, can you. Even a poor orphaned bitch like Trini is open season to you!

Alex: I'm sure that if a Martian landed here tomorrow, he or she of it would approve of the shape of your bottom.

Jane: Say it again please.

Alex: He stroke, she stroke, it would approve of the shape of your…bottom. But might make the observation and find it strange that the human race totally breeds and controls its livestock, horses, cattle, sheep, pigs, chickens and the rest, yet takes no action over its own breeding stock. Weird, isn't it.

Jane: But we are not cattle!

Alex: Some would argue that point. But hey, Godless Sister, we are animals, are we not.

Jane: Don't keep calling me that!

Alex: For today you are the Godless Sister…Alright, I know, Adolf and the Nazis gave eugenics a bad name and since the end of the Second World War no nation will dare tackle the problem staring us all plain in the face. All the **free** transistor radios in the world ain't gonna make a blind bit of difference. Since I was at school the world's population has nearly doubled in twenty-five years. We will soon not have nearly enough food, clean water, medicines, even clean air to go around. Simple!

Jane: What do you propose then, that all couples take up anal sex like us. We would all be locked up!

Alex: Smart words snaking around! By Grand Central Station I sat down and cried. Recently voted the worst novel ever written…Later, Godless Sister, later…

(The upstairs lounge door opens and Nurse Susan bursts into the flat.)

Susan: Dorothy is all ready to go. She's washed, dressed and expectant. Your boy, Ben, is here as well. I'm sorry, my loves, but IO have to go. I'm promised to meet Desi at ten o'clock sharp. All under control. Is there anything else you need me to do before I leave?

(Nurse Susan winks knowingly ay Alex in a flirtatious manner a split-second before Jane enters hurriedly from the open-doored bedroom, still pulling a jumper on over her head and half-colliding with a table.)

Jane: Ouch! That really hurt!...Thank you, Susan. Now, you will be back here for nine o'clock tonight, won't you?...Good. I just could not handle the whole day on my own. It sounds selfish, I know. Self-preservation, I guess. Alex here has a theory based on the lowest common denominator principle. In other words, we all sink down to a basic level rather than rise up. *(Laughs girlishly.)* Mental illness and its attendant side-effects attacks all healthy-minded people and is unsettling...I just do not know how you cope with it, Susan. You are truly a nursing angel.

Susan: That's not what my Desi says about me, Jane love. *(Susan turns in th3e act of responding and smiles too warmly at a motionless Alex.)* I don't let it touch me, my loves. It's outside of my control, see. I just do it. We all get there in the end if we are lucky enough. I don't think about it too much. I have my family and my own life to leaf. Now, if you will excuse me, I must away otherwise Desi will get very angry and when Desi gets...

Jane: Thank you, Susan, that is very good of you.

(Nurse Susan leaves, shooting a quick glance at Alex. Trini the dog is barking incessantly. The church bells are chiming again. Alex goes over and stands up close behind Jane, folding his arms around her neck and shoulders, pushing up tight against her bottom.)

Alex: There goes Nurse Susan, all neat and tidy in her starched uniform and displaying signs of Cornish sex appeal, thinking you wouldn't notice.

Jane: I didn't notice a thing. I think it is all in your dirty mind. You see sexual motives behind everything.

(Alex pressing even tighter against Jane.)

Alex: I'm not alone, Miss Freud...Christ, the noise level here is just manic. That dog should be shot! Sorry. I know. The apple and glow of your blue-tinted eyes. Those bloody birds sound like they are getting ready to attack. The cry of seagulls scratching at the sapphire-blue sky.

(Jane grasps Alex's hand over her chest. Sighs. Looks wistfully out pf the lounge flat window at the church spire and the sea. Moves her bottom involuntarily in a sexual motion against Alex. Sighs again.)

Alex: Your sigh sounds soft like summer rain.

Act 2

Scene: Inside a car containing four occupants. Alex Croy is driving. Jane is in the front passenger seat. A ten year old, angelic-looking, blonde-haired, blue-eyed boy, Ben, is sat behind. Also, Mum/Dorothy is sat directly behind Jane. The car is moving.)

Jane: Look out, that workman is about to step out in front of us!

(Alex Croy swerves the car around a sneering, young guy who has opened a white van back door to it's maximum limit and is leering aggressively at the rich funks from the house on the hill as they drive on past.)

Alex: Straw Dogs lives!

Jane: Sssh! You should drive more carefully. It is dangerous. This is not an auspicious start...Did you see that, Mum? That stupid young workman almost walked straight into us.

Dorothy: What, dear?

Jane: Didn't you see it!...Oh, never mind. Have you got everything you need?

Dorothy: What do I need then?

Jane: Well, I don't really know. I guess I'm making an undue fuss because I am excited for you.

Alex: You mean you are excited for yourself. This is your trip and you know it. Isn't that right, Ben?

(Ben stares quietly out of the car window.)

Jane: Don't try and draw poor Ben into your mind games, Alex Croy. Or is it Ashley Croy today? I almost forgot!

Alex: you know damn well that Ashley is my writing and working name.

(Alex is fiddling using his left hand with the cassette holder on the car radio and sound system. He hits the play button and Canned Heat's 'Let's Work Together' blasts out across the interior of the car.)

Jane: *(shouting)* For goodness sake, turn that music down...Turn it down!

(Jane fingers frantically at the volume control and turns it up full blast by mistake. Panics and hastily switches the cassette player off altogether.)

Alex: Killjoy.

Jane: Thank you! Not a good way to start a journey. You could deafen Mum completely. And anyway, I hate all that old-fashioned sixties type of music. Did you notice that as we pulled out onto the main road people were staring at us?

Alex: I'm not surprised; you turned it up full blast. Proper Bob the Bear fan, aren't we?

Jane: What?

Alex: Nothing.

Jane: I do so hate it when you do that. You use knowledge, any kind of knowledge, as a weapon. Just because I do not know the names and the in-crowd clues and gossip from long ago, you treat me as if I am some kind of straight fool. A Miss Stuck-up, No-nothing. You are superior in a cruel way about so-called, hip information.

Alex: Let me get this right. *(Driving with one hand on the steering wheel and playing with the car radio with the other at the same time.)* Aren't you the qualified teacher around here with a degree who argued with me that Moscow is in Asia?

Jane: Geography was never a strong subject of mine.

Alex: Really. *(Tuning in the car radio which is cranking out the latest BBC news bulletin.)*

Car radio: News of fresh atrocities reported in Bosnia has just reached us.

Jane: Please turn that off. It upsets me so to continually hear depressing news all of the time...You do not want to hear that, Mum, do you?

(Dorothy looks blank then realises that she is expected to respond.)

Dorothy: I like music, dear.

Jane: You do not want to hear this news, Ben, do you?

(Ben shakes his head ever so slightly as the news bulletin continues.)

Jane: You see, you are outvoted by three to one. We do not want to hear this ugly news.

Alex: Who said this is a democracy.

Jane: Look out! Mind that car!...God!

Alex: That's why you wear glasses and I possess twenty-twenty vision. There was enough room to have got a Bosnian bus through that gap...Who told you this was a democracy and anyway doesn't Dorothy want to hear more of Canned Heat.

Jane; I think she would rather listen to music of her own time like the thirties.

(Alex moves the car radio dial away from the news bulletin.)

Alex: Name some thirties musicians then.

Jane: You know full well that I can't. Why should I know anything about music of the thirties anyway?

Alex: The Roy Fox Band, Al Bowlly, Lew Stone, Noel Coward, Ambrose...

Jane: Smart arse...Sorry, Mum.

Alex: Now, while we are talking of smart...

Jane: Don't you just dare! This is Mum's day out. Can't you just let it be for once. Can't we simply just relax and enjoy the ride...And I know full well who Noel Coward is, thank you very much!

Alex: Good. Just remember, if it wasn't for bad news there wouldn't be any news at all.

Jane: Do you have to drive do fast? Exactly how quickly are we going?

Alex: A safe seventy all of the way.

Jane: And the rest! You will get us all killed!

Alex: Confidence, dear, confidence. You know full well I am an advanced driver and I have the certificate to prove it. And anyway, this car was made to cruise at ninety...Everybody happy? You bet your life we are...Are you okay, Dorothy?

(Dorothy looks up and smiles at the back of Alex's head. Not making any eye contact with his eyes in the driving mirror.)

Dorothy: Yes, thank you, dear.

Alex: Ben?

(Ben sits smiling behind Alex's neck and continues looking out of the car window at the scrub Cornish countryside flashing by.)

Alex: Good! Then we are all just one big, happy family.

Jane: You never asked me if I was all right. Just took it for granted.

Alex: Okay, Godless Sister, a mere oversight…Are you enjoying yourself do far on this lovely summer's day?

Jane: Please don't start calling me that again in front of Mum and Ben. I really do not like it. I'm worried that I didn't telephone and double-check with the Bensons to make sure they are expecting us.

Alex: I'm surprised we ever managed to get out of the house and into the car at all. That mad bitch Trini almost barked the house down. Did you hear her throwing her body against the inside of the flat door as we were leaving? Thud! Crack! At least that sneering young guy with the white van will think twice about trying to rob us…You are always finding something to worry about. Remember that Austrian student we had staying last summer? He was always going on about English people and the worry lines they have etched between their eyebrows. I'd never ever thought about it before. But when I started to look hard I noticed that nearly every other person I looked at had those worry lines, including you, Godless Sister.

Jane: Please, I said…Trini can't help it. She just wanted to come with us, that's all… She's a part of the family and felt excluded…I did not like that Austrian student, Joseph, one bit. He turned out to be very smug. Looking down on us when he had nothing really to be so superior about.

Alex: How's your Austrian then?

Jane: *(Ignoring the taunt.)* Maybe you could look out for a phone box where we could stop and I could call the Bensons. Though I'm not so sure I've got their number with me.

Alex: How do you do it, Miss Godless Sister? You could be Lizzie Borden on a mission for all they know or Myra Hindley let out on parole.

Jane: Stop it! Not in front of Ben, please.

Alex: Let me get this right! You ring up total strangers and get there attention by telling them all about Dorothy. How the farm had been in her family for three generations. How she grew up there and lived there until she was twenty-three. About her condition.

How, if we could just visit, it would be so very nice and Dorothy might somehow remember w3jho she really was...And, hey presto, they say yes and invite us to lunch. Just like that as the Egyptian fez fell on the floor laughing. We are total strangers from out of the Cornish mists and these Bensons are going to open up their farm doors to us without even a second thought. Truly, Godless Sister, you are a magic lady. I don't know how you do it. Sacred plums just roll right off your tongue and the sun smiles with pleasure.

(It is starting to rain, very heavily.)

Jane: Was that a flash of lightning? God!

Alex: There's your answer. The God of Thunder has spoken and is less than five miles from us.

Jane: Slow down. Will you please slow down! How can you see to dftrive4 in this torrential rain?

Alex: Three-speed windscreen wipers. Just watch level three goes.

Jane: But they are moving so rapidly they're not eve4n clearing the windscreen properly...Please slow down, Alex. This is scary. Another flash of lightning. Did you see it! It's alright, Mum. We are all quite safe.

Alex: Look, I've slowed down as instructed. The God of Thunder has moved away from us. Hotfooted it down Plymouth way. He's had about enough of the confines of Redruth. Go out for a night on the tiles in Redruth and paint the town blue.

Jane: I've said it before, Alex, you are just not funny. You do not possess the funny gene.

Alex: Dorothy was completely unmoved by it all...You okay, Ben?

(Ben smiles quietly.)

Alex: It has all cleared up just as fast as it came. Are you happy again, Godless Sister? Is normal service resumed?

Jane: Did I hear you say that you are writing a piece about Mum and her condition?

Alex: And Auntie as well.

Jane: Has it got a title?

Alex: The Planet Can Be A Lonely Place Sometimes.

Jane:	Ummm. That is quite good. I trust you are carefully disguising Mum and Auntie's identities?
Alex:	What will they care?
Jane:	I care. It affects me, the boys, Stephen and Ben, nephews and nieces, aunts and uncles. You have to think of the affect upon other people. You just can't go writing about people, it is disquieting. It will unsettle the family and all of our friends and set them wondering if it might well happen to them one day.
Alex:	All good art is meant to be disquieting. Disturbing…The thunder and lightning has stopped, Dorothy. All cleared up in a flash.
Dorothy:	Yes, dear.
Jane:	Don't do that please. You are a dispassionate bastard. Sorry, Mum, please excuse my French. You are playing games again. You did that deliberately to concoct a line in your planned article, essay, short story, whatever, I suppose…The planet is a…what was it?
Alex:	All together now, one more time. The planet can be a lonely place sometimes.

(It is now raining and the sun is shining both at the very same time.)

Jane:	Look, Ben, there is a rainbow. Can you see it?

(Ben smiles serenely and nods.)

Alex:	It's a monkey's wedding.
Jane:	What?
Alex:	Christ! You heard exactly what I said. Why do I continually have to repeat everything that I say? It's like I'm explaining to the hard of hearing, a group of confused Chinese students or a party of autistic children on a special school outing to Cornwall for the day…Monkey's wedding. Monkey's wedding. Monkey's wedding.
Jane:	Isn't he cruel, Mum?
Dorothy:	*(puzzled)* Yes, dear…Where are the monkeys? I cannot see any.
Jane:	See, what you have gone and done! You have confused, Mum.

Alex: Godless Sister, you are staring at me like I'm evoking the Scopes Monkey Trial of Nineteen-Twenties America. You want me to talk about Clarence Darrow?

Jane: No, thank you and please refrain from any more references to our simian friends. Can't you see it perturbs Mum?

Alex: That's a quaint way of putting it. Talking about our ancestors as friends with red quotation marks implied around the pronunciation. Take heed, Ben. You may well need some of this information for your future biology lessons in a few years time. This could well be an opportune moment to discuss the Scopes monkey trial. He was only a simple teacher, just like you, Godless Sister. Teaching Darwin's Theory of Evolution in the Southern Bible-bashing belt of America in the nineteen-twenties. White-hooded folks got quite upset. Related to the apes. My God, Mister, whatever next! You must be mad, a plain demented fool and no mistake, Mister...And all I said was it's a monkey's wedding which, as everybody well knows, Godless Sister, simply means that the sun is shining and it is raining all at the same time...Sorry, Dorothy, no monkeys dancing in the Cornish trees or dangling on the beautifully streaked rainbow. And anyway, the precious moment has passed. The thundering rain has moved on to torment other God-fearing Clarence Darrow detractors and you, being a fully paid-up member of the Teaching Union and all, Miss Godless Sister. And before you answer that with an absurd question, let me state very clearly that we are all going straight to hell in a rolling handcart.

Jane: How dare you, in front of Mum and Ben! You have no right! Put on a cassette, play with the radio if you must...Just what were you thinking of?

Alex: Sorry.

Jane: Did I hear you right? That must be the very first time you have apologised to me so far this year. I heard it clearly, but I really cannot quite believe it.

Alex: I was just trying to somehow manoeuvre Sidney Carton and Clarence Darrow intro the same sentence, but it didn't quite work. But hey there, Miss Godless Sister, I humbly grovel before your sweet voluptuous...

Jane: Sssh! Don't! Please! Let us just enjoy the journey and try and be friends for at least the next five minutes...Would you like some chocolate, Mum?...Ben?...

Alex: Simply a tale of two monkeys.

Jane: I've told you before, you are not funny and, of course, you will not deign to eat a piece of chocolate with us. Denying yourself a pleasure just to stay lean and mean.

Alex: It's all just for you, Godless Sister. You get to feel my rippling pectoral muscles...Heave ho and away we go.

(Alex starts once again to play with the dial on the car radio. Suddenly he lets out a strangulated murmur...)

Alex: Immm...

(...of satisfaction as cricket commentary starts broadcasting on the car radio from Test Match Special Commentary.)

Car radio: And Atherton plays a magnificent square cut as England make a good start here in Nottingham today. Maybe third time lucky and England can turn things around in this Test Match, Trevor...I seriously doubt it somehow, Brian...

Jane: Oh God, not the cricket! That will drive me plumb crazy if I have to listen to this for the rest of the journey to Salcombe. Anything but the cricket! And you are supposed to possess fine taste and discriminatory powers of discernment. Why, I discovered you upstairs in the flat the other week watching cricket when you should have been working. Drooling over some fat, dyed-blonde Australian and trying to tell me he is beautiful and a genius. I really thought you had lost it altogether.

(Alex turns the volume on the Test Match cricket commentary down very low.)

Alex: You don't begin to understand, Godless Sister. He is beautiful. He is a very special leg break, googly bowler with a wickedly deceptive top spinner...Don't frown so. You will only develop permanent crow's feet under your eyes and then where will we be? I shan't any longer be able to send you out to work at night.

Jane: Stop it! Ben is in the car as you well know and Mum sometimes picks up on things when you least expect it.

Alex: Sorry...Ooops, there I go again, twice in one day. That's because you were so deliciously wicked with me earlier this morning...They say, whoever they are, that beauty is in the eye of the beholder. It is. But just the same, what you do can make you truly wonderful... Was Dame Margot Fonteyn a radiant beauty? Did Maria Callas's darks looks launch a thousand ships? No cracks please about Greek shipping magnates, Jane. Oh, I quite forgot. That is just not your style, is it. We are coy, suppressed, English roses and we float serenely above the oily, choppy waters...What you do can make you beautiful. This guy, Warne, is a throwback to a bygone age, a genius and he is pure magic to watch. It grieves me to say so as an English supporter, but there is no denying class...You're frowning again. The crow's feet are on the march again...By the way, see, I've turned the radio down low especially for you, Godless Sister...Is your American friend, Emily, beautiful? I heard they are all bonkers in Yankees.

Jane:	I do admit she is on the large side.
Alex:	Prime English understatement if ever I heard it and, by the way, England are suddenly sixty-three for two and that man, Warne, has got Atherton right on cue. You see, I don't just make it up to bamboozle you, Godless Sister...Your New Yorker friend, Emily, with the Callipygian bottom, keeps trying to chat me up on the sly.
Jane:	You're lying and please keep your voice down and don't say bottom...Are you all right, Mum?...If you must, turn that cricket back up, but...
Alex:	Okay, okay. Keep your crow's feet in place. That American Emily claims she's your best friend. That's day last week when she came over making gooey eyes at me on the sly, wetting her large, sensuous lips with her darting tongue. She can sense the way we like to do it and kept turning her ample bottom, sorry, in my direction and openly offering...
Jane:	Sssh! Will you please change the subject! I do not believe it. You are always trying to turn me against my friends. When I first met you I had plenty of friends, but your caustic sarcasm and abrupt manner has turned them all away except for Emily, and now you try to poison me against her. You are so very cruel, utterly selfish and quite heartless. You are using this situation to get at me because you know very well I cannot respond accordingly and anyway, Emily...
Alex:	Shot Stewie!...I kid you not about American Emily. I haven't turned any of your fair-weather friends against you. Most of them are just plain jealous. Not one of them is in a successful relationship. P2 is a veritable coven of suppressed lesbians, cackling and gossiping. Controlling and dominating. They can laugh and sneer. Most of the men around just shutdown because they coexist in a drunken daze. The women control the purse strings and feel intellectually superior to their poor, inferior, stupid men. So saying with the sniping, precious, P2 coven, anyone who dares stand up to them intellectually and emotionally they pretend to despise and criticise whilst secretly craving fantasies with themselves placed right at the heart of

these wishful daydreams. They're envious of you, that's all. That American Emily, your so-called best friend, just cannot bring herself to believe that I would not prefer her so-cool and penetrating self to you...Christ, Stewie is on top form today. Great! But hey, I bet that Warney gets him.

(The sun is now shining very brightly on the car windscreen. Jane has put on a pair of dark glasses.)

Jane: I do not know how you can see to drive in this glaring sunshine...How long before we reach Plymouth?...Not much longer, Ben, and you will be able to get out and stretch your legs...Are you all right, Mum? Do you need to use the toilet? We can stop whenever you like.

Dorothy: I am quite all right, thank you, dear.

(Ben has got his blonde-haired head buried deep in a comic book.)

Jane: You've switched the cricket off. What is this music?

Alex: Just to see you smile, Godless Sister. Just to see you smile. I heard tell somewhere that Mozart is the most soothing of music. They, the infamous Grey Folk again, carried out experiments in different mental institutions in and around the Bristol area and found out that Mozart's music seemed to create the most peaceful and calming of atmospheres.

Jane: Are you saying that we all need calming down?

Alex: Yes, if you must ask. But really I just wanted to see you smile for once. Even from behind those old-fashioned shades. You hardly ever smile. I shall now always remember you smiling across time...I only really like Mozart played in a minor key, clarinet and oboe in a minor key like this.

Jane: Wait. Wait. Not so fast please. You always do that to me...Nearly there, Ben...You say something that cuts sharp then move on quickly to another subject before I even have time to digest the implications of your words. Always trying to keep one step ahead of me. Constantly striving to throw me off balance. You want to remember me smiling across time? But that implies we have no future now. Are you planning on leaving me after today?...Sorry, Mum. It is alright. We are not arguing.

(Dorothy is looking alarmed and becoming increasingly agitated.)

Dorothy: What is it? Where are you taking me?

Jane: See what you have done. You have gone and upset Mum with your oh so clever words. And anyway, how can you truly remember my smile across time if I am wearing dark glasses. You are perverse. You know that, Alex Croy, don't you?

Alex: We are taking you home to the farm outside of Salcombe where you grew up, Dorothy. Do you remember?

Dorothy: I do not really know, dear.

Alex: Well, never mind, Dorothy. We shall soon traverse Plymouth, the black hole of the south-west. Scoot across the Tamar Bridge and be flying down to Salcombe with Dolores del Rio.

Jane: What are you saying?

Alex: Throwing out old names and images in the hope that something might just hit. Disturb a memory. Create a reaction.

Jane: But you know full well that can never happen.

Alex: If you say so, Godless Sister, if you say so.

Jane: The doctors definitely said there is no recall whatsoever after a while. All memories are washed clean away. But we live in hope, Mum, don't we?

(Dorothy has a blank look, nil response.)

Alex: But they don't really know, do they? Every case must be of individual concern. That's the trouble with living in an age obsessed with statistics. A thousand studied cases had no sign of any memory recall then it must always be so. The death of the individual. Dorothy may well be different.

Jane: If only you were right. But you are wrong and you know very well that you are...I thought this music was supposed to be soothing. It just seems to be making you even more cantankerous than normal.

Alex: Mark Twain would not agree with you.

Jane: Oh, not that old chestnut again about statistics and damned lies, please. The same old people are always trotted out and quoted. You pretend to be ultra modern and cutting edge, but you are just as bad. Go on, remind me again who the obvious ones are...We shall soon be there, Mum, no need to worry.

(Dorothy looks blank and is uncomfortable. She knows she should somehow respond, but does not understand what is expected of her.)

Alex: The other candidates beside Mark Twain?...Well, there's Ralph Waldo Emerson, Oscar Wilde, George Bernard Shaw, Noel Coward, Dorothy Parker and Harry S. Truman. Aren't they the ones you mean, Godless Sister?

Jane: If you say so, Alex, then they are the ones. What was Truman famous for?

Alex: We're back to Moscow being in Asia again, are we not, Teacher?

Jane: Don't! You know full well that politics and geography are not strong subjects of mine.

Alex: Don't get all steamed up and stuffy behind those dark glasses of yours...There's the River Tamar, Ben. The dividing boundary between Cornwall and Devon. The difference between scrub country and rich pastoral land...Harry S. Truman, the thirty-third President of the United States of America, Godless Sister, was, is, most famous for 'Fat Man' and 'Little Boy'. They were the names given to the atomic bombs that were dropped on Hiroshima and Nagasaki.

Act 3

Scene: A large stone farmhouse set deep in the richly green, rolling countryside of Devon. Situated ten miles or so inland from Salcombe. Jane is stood in the garden at the rear of the farmhouse, with her are Leslie and Marianne Benson. Alex, Dorothy and Ben linger behind Jane.)

Jane: It really is so very wonderful of you to see us like this. Words almost fail me. I am so excited. This is a real trip down memory lane for me, but as you can well imagine, the memories are lodged in the stories my mother told to me when I was a young girl. This is the very first time that I have ever been here…How old were you when Glebe Farm was sold, Mum?

(Dorothy remains blank-faced and silent.)

Jane: Oh, never mind, Mum, it will come back to you. That is the point of today's journey really, Leslie, Marianne. I feel I already know you both well enough to call you by your Christian names. You have been so very kind to us already.

Marianne: Think nothing of it, Jane. It must be an awful experience for you. Quite painful…We had a distant cousin, didn't we, Leslie, one day doing just fine and dandy and extremely busy, then the next…*(Snaps her fingers dramatically.)* Totally withdrawn. Not able to interact or operate within society at all. No longer aware of anyone or anything. He was dead within eighteen months…Oh, I am so awfully sorry, Jane! There I go again, putting my great big fat foot right in it.

Leslie: That is why, folks, I am the PR consultant and Marianne specialises in flower arranging.

Alex: Don't concern yourself, Marianne. I have already made a thousand and one mistakes since I first prised open my sticky eyes this morning. Jane has cursed me to hell and beyond since we first drew back the bedroom curtains on the morning to the sound of wretched seagulls screeching.

(Jane shifts uncomfortably on her garden chair and immediately changes the subject.)

Jane: But now Glebe Farm is called Treetops Farm and that is truly amazing, isn't it, Mum?

(Dorothy looks worried, but says nothing.)

Jane: You see, as a young girl, we had a summer cottage near Rye in Sussex called Treetops.

Alex: Which, of course, is an unusual name.

(Jane plows on, ignoring the implied sarcasm.)

Jane: Isn't that strange. We used to summer there, Mum, Dad, Auntie and me, until I was about twelve years old. Dad sold it for a considerable profit and we started holidaying in Cornwall instead. Which is how Dad came to buy the present house. Odd coincidence...Alex likes to refer to us as blow-ins.

(Marianne has disappeared inside the farmhouse and reappears shortly with a large tray containing plates of separate cut cheese and cucumber sandwiches, Madeira cake, chocolate biscuits and a large pot of English tea. All complete with china cups, saucers, plates, knives, spoons, milk, sugar and serviettes.)

Jane: Oh, you should not have gone to all this trouble, Marianne. How extremely kind of you.

Leslie: Of course, the farmland has been sold off separately long ago and I believe there was another name change between Glebe Farm and Treetops.

Marianne; Would you like a sandwich...Sorry, I've forgotten...

Jane: Ben...And he must have read that comic at least three times today already. Marianne is offering you a sandwich, Ben, answer please.

(Ben glances up from his head buried deep in the comic. Smiles beautifully at Marianne and takes a proffered cheese sandwich.)

Jane: Thank you, please, Ben. Manners.

Ben: *(smiling shyly)* Thanks.

Marianne: Oh, don't worry yourself, Jane. I was painfully shy at the self-same age...Do you really think this visit will help your mother?

Jane: Well, I really hope so. This is a lovely garden. Funny, until today I had never ever realised how much I missed Treetops. Oh, I did so adore and savour our summer holidays there. It was like being in a perpetual summer wonderland. The summers seemed to always last forever. The sun always shone or so it seemed. But when it rained it was even better. Tucked up safe, reading my favourite books sat in the conservatory with my legs stretched out on a couch and the long running drops of rain playing on the giant panes of glass.

Alex: Very poetic.

Jane: Do you remember Treetops, Mum?...Mum...Where is Mum? She's completely vanished!

Leslie: Maybe this visit has somehow triggered her memory and she has gone to look for some of her old haunts. Her childhood bedroom perhaps?

Jane: Oh, I do so hope you are right, Leslie...Ben, please wipe those breadcrumbs from your lips...Be an absolute angel, dear, and go inside the house and see if you can locate your grandmother.

Marianne: I will go with him, Jane. Of course, this farmhouse has been completely redesigned and renovated since your mother...Dorothy?...

(Alex nods.)

Marianne: ...lived here. But she has probably gone upstairs to see for herself...Smells and tastes, Jane. They always help to surrender up memories, don't they?

Alex: Maybe we should all have dunked madeleines instead this afternoon.

Jane: *(covering up her annoyance)* That is the writer in him, Leslie, being clever, witty and sharp.

(Blonde-haired Ben reluctantly raises his head from out of his comic book again and slowly follows Marianne into the farmhouse.)

Jane: *(fidgeting nervously and making small talk)* What do you find to do, stuck way out here, Leslie? It must have been quite a wrench, leaving London.

Leslie: I have my own PR consultancy, Jane. Marianne and I have always loved this part of the world. We saved hard then, as luck would have it, this farmhouse came onto the market just as we were looking.

(Marianne reappears with Ben trailing behind her. She is showing some slight degree of concern.

Marianne: Your mother, Dorothy, is nowhere to be seen in the farmhouse, Jane. We called out for her repeatedly, but nothing. She seems to have totally vanished.

Jane: Are you absolutely sure?

Leslie: Maybe the rich scent of these rosebushes has reignited in her thoughts of some long-forgotten favourite walk. She will be back soon, I am sure. It just proves how vital and therapeutic it is to take people back to where they grew up. It was good of you, Jane, to make such an effort...The previous owners said there had always been these rosebushes here. Probably planted by Dorothy's grandfather, I shouldn't wonder. You don't lose those sort of connections, they are inherent in the soul. A part of the special condition of being. They will continue to resurface at some point if triggered by an experience or relived sense. Just like your visit here today. I do congratulate you both.

Jane: Well, I do so thank you for that, Leslie. It is because of you and Marianne...Alex, will you do me a special favour, please?

Alex: And what act would you like me to perform for you, Jane?

Jane: *(reddening in the face, but plowing on regardless)* Please go and look for Mum. She cannot have gone very far. Probably gravitated towards some favourite spot from the past. In all likelihood, it has all come flooding back and entirely overwhelmed her.

Scene: Alex rises from his garden chair and casually sidles out. Walks back inside the farmhouse. Eventually, after five minutes of searching around, Alex finds a confused and agitated Dorothy standing on her own in the lane outside the front entrance to the newly-named Treetops Farm. She has no idea of who she is or where she is.

(Alex touches Dorothy's shoulder.)

Dorothy: I want to go home...I want to go home...

(Alex leads a confused and dismayed Dorothy back into the rear garden.)

Dorothy: *(to no-one in particular)* I want to go home!

Jane: *(smiling, relieved)* But you are home, Mum. Don't you remember?

Dorothy: I do not know this place. I want to go home, do you hear!

(Dorothy starts a temper tantrum. Stamps her foot angrily. Starting to show signs of agitated aggression.)

Jane: But you grew up here, Mum!

Dorothy: *(getting angrier now)* I have never been here before in my life. Now take me home at once!

(Confusion now studies Dorothy's face. The energy and anger have suddenly passed. Jane is embarrassed before the Bensons who are so considerate and so caring which makes it ten times worse. A sudden, squally shower of rain.)

Leslie: Quick, gather up your teacups, folks, and run for the cover of the conservatory.

Alex: *(standing in the conservatory, holding a teapot and the lid)* This is April kind of weather and I guess that makes you an April kind of girl, Jane.

Jane: *(clutching onto the arm of a dismayed Dorothy who has been dragged into the conservatory out of the showering rain)* Whatsoever do you mean, Alex Croy? Springtime, April, represents changeability and all the seasons that can flow through a day at once.

Alex: Exactly…I saw the best girls of my generation destroyed by manners, starving, hysterical, naked.

(Marianne giggles in a playfully sexual manner. Flirts ostentatiously, holding her china cup of tea in one hand with her little finger crooked free and waves a soggy-looking cucumber sandwich in the other.)

Alex: The bruising pleasures of the flesh.

Jane: Pardon me?

Alex: Spinning thoughts just springing right off my mindful tongue…I guess the sleep spindle of time has spun long-forgotten memories clean out of Dorothy's head.

Marianne: I can tell you are a writer, Alex. You are so very lucky to be living with an artist, Jane. It must be so inspiring.

Jane: Oh, it is, Marianne. It is. You can have no idea.

Marianne: *(warming to the conversation)* And what is the main theme of your writing, Alex?

Alex: *(contriving to ignore frantic warning signals from Jane)* I don't really have a continuous theme, do I, Jane? It changes from day to day. Hour by hour. At this precise moment, with my feet planted firmly in this beautiful garden, in the rain, the sea edging towards us on the breeze, I feel underpinning all of my work is the idea and belief that we are all just dead people on shore leave. That we will all soon return to the ocean of the unconscious from whence we all came.

Leslie: Do you have other constant themes that keep recurring, Alex? I would like to know.

Alex: Well, in the immortal words of Hassan I Sabbath, the Grand Master of the Assassins, nothing is true, everything is permitted.

(Jane shifts her bottom uncomfortably on her conservatory garden chair. Nervously, her blue eyes resettle on the Bensons' rosebushes in full bloom.)

Jane: If only we had rosebushes like that in our gardens in Cornwall. The scent of the roses alone wafting around in here is making me quite giddy with pleasure.

Leslie: *(smiling)* We feel the same, Jane. Though it is always good to be reminded of the beauty of them…Would it be appropriate to ask you outright about Alzheimer's disease and the ongoing effects?

Jane: Mum won't mind. It seems to all be passing straight over her head…*(gulping)*…It is a condition, illness, that steals your very life from out under you. Robs you of all your precious memories. It is like someone has destroyed every photograph of you that has ever existed.

Marianne: Oh Jane!

Jane: It completely wipes out any hope of a future. Any thought of reading and basic communication go clean out of the window. Family and friends totally disappear, as if they had never, ever existed. Even failing sometimes to recognise your own daughter…

(Jane wipes away a dignified tear.)

Leslie: That must be a really awful experience, Jane. God, I hope that never, ever happens to us!

Alex: One in five chance, we are told, should we ever hit seventy. Supposing, that is, we ever get that far.

Jane: The calming voice of artistic concern. You are so reassuring, Alex.

Alex: *(grinning before the accusing eyes of Marianne)* Just stating our chances as we know them at present, that's all.

(Jane abruptly stands up.)

Jane: Ben, would you be an absolute angel and take your dear grandmother out to the car. She looks very tired now. She seems quite ready for a nap. It has been a very long day already.

(Blonde-haired Ben sticks his comic under his arm. Takes his now passive grandmother by the hand as he accepts the car keys from Alex with his other hand.)

Alex: On second thoughts, I'll go with them, just make sure everything is okay.

Marianne: Oh, do please come back, Alex. I will make a fresh pot of tea for you.

(Alex follows a blonde-haired Ben, gently leading his grandmother, Dorothy, out of the conservatory and through the wet garden. It is still raining lightly.)

Jane: *(becoming very animated before her captive conservatory audience of the Bensons)* Of course, Alzheimer's the illness is bad enough in itself, but for the relatives, it is very hard to deal with. The constant daily reminder of hurt and pain just does your head in. It finally gets to you, no matter how strong-willed and detached you are about it. My father, Sid, suffered with the daily trials and tribulations and never-ending worry, for two whole years and more...Yes, I will have another cup of tea, thank you, Marianne...My father was living in our big house in Cornwall with Mum and Auntie. They both seemed to show extended symptoms of the disease at the self-same time. Sid, my poor father, must have been panic-stricken. Acting in secret, poor darling. Afraid that the world would find out. Shame haunts us all, doesn't it. You must understand how cruel life can be in a small Cornish fishing village. You are always strangers even if you have lived there twenty-five years. You are still considered outsiders or, in Alex's phrase, blow-ins. The village tongues never stop wagging. We all trooped over to my parents' house for Christmas dinner, eighteen or so months ago. Alex, the boys and I. Dad had insisted that Mum cook the Christmas dinner. Auntie was kept well out of the way upstairs. The whole event turned into a complete fiasco. Mum, poor darling, attempted to serve up half-cooked and frozen food. She had no knowledge whatsoever of what she was about, poor dear. In her heyday, she was such a marvellous cook, you know. Dad tried hard to hide his embarrassment. Making a show of Mum's lamentable efforts as a severe winter cold with her prescribed, medicine producing strange, forgetful side effects. Alex made matters worse by taking great delight in over-pronouncing the word botulism. Dad could have killed him. I cooked us up a hasty dinner and told the boys their grandmother had a bad case of flu. We do not know what to believe. You just do not want to accept the possibility, you know. The idea of Alzheimer's disease carries such a stigma even today. Then there is the awful thought that it could well be you some day. The family connection. I looked at the boys playing cricket with Alex out by the church wall garden and shivered with fright. All the while Dad is making excuses. Carrying on the pretence. Through it all, Mum just sat there, smiling. Nothing else, no comment, just sat smiling…Later, I think it was on the same visit, I went upstairs and found Auntie talking to Alex. I was shocked to see she had the makings of a full-grown moustache. She was vaguely telling Alex that she had seen the Queen Mary that morning sail past the window of her upstairs flat. Sailing right on by the superimposed image of the village church spire. It was then I knew for certain that they were both completely losing it…I do not know the exact dates, Alex will know, he stores everything like that. I will ask him when he comes back, but the Queen Mary has not sailed to America these thirty years past. I am certain. The only good thing, I suppose, about it all was that Auntie could still, at that stage, recall seeing the Queen Mary…You see, the speed of the decline is not in a straight line, it varies incredibly…Can you imagine being caught up in a situation like that! Pretending to the world at large that everything is all right. Not prepared to accept the idea of illness. Those two batty old women, my mother and Auntie, slowly wore him down. Drained all his energy. He would not even let on to me, his only daughter. Never confided in anyone. Kept it all to himself. That generation were tough like that yet also closed off. Not able to let their feelings through. Unable to express their real emotions. I suppose a part of it was having to live and fight through the second world war. He was a true working class man, my father, Sid. A self-employed plumber who built up his own successful business from absolutely nothing. A self-made man in all respects, if you like. Rose from the poverty of the poorhouse to being rich all through his own hard-fought efforts. He was fully aware of the class divide…I am so sorry, Leslie, Marianne, I am going on about my own family, I just cannot stop once I start talking about the family happenings, they just keep tumbling out. I'm sorry…

Leslie: Carry on, Jane, it is good for you. Helps deal with the anguish and the pain.

Jane: Thank you both. You are so very kind. It is just the thought of my father, Sid, doing all the washing, ironing, cooking, cleaning, shopping, living the lie to the whole world. Living in fear that somebody someday would find out. Reveal his deadly secret. What he actually thought, I do not know. I never ever found any books or pamphlets lying around the house on Alzheimer's disease, dementia or senility. Both Mum and Auntie were a few years older than him, you see. They came from an upper

	middle class Devonian farm family. My mother came out as a debutante and was presented to the local society. That would have been in the early nineteen thirties. Salcombe was the centre for quite a high-class society in those days for this part of the world. It probably still is for all I know.
Leslie:	Still the same, my dear.
Jane:	A social elite and my mother was the belle of the ball. Nineteen thirty-three, I should guess. God, she was so attractive. I still have the photographs, so fashionable. Her family were numbered among the first farm families in this area.
Marianne:	Oh, isn't that so sad to think that Dorothy was once the belle of the ball...I mean, I didn't...
Leslie:	Marianne!
Marianne:	Sorry, Jane.
Jane:	Oh, it doesn't matter.
Marianne:	I am way past worrying about that sort of thing...One Friday, nearly seven months ago to the day, Dad was in Penzance early for some shopping and business. He would leave Mum and Auntie behind, locking them in. Shut off the gas and trust the rest to luck. Keeping up appearances. Probably never knew what he was likely to come back to. That Friday he parked the car in the town car park and got as far as the Humphrey Davy statue in Market Jew Street. Nine o'clock in the morning, striking on the town clock. He had a heart attack and collapsed. Fell down dead in the street, right at the base of the Humphrey Davy statue.
Marianne:	Oh Jane!
Jane:	He was pronounced dead in the ambulance on the way to the hospital, but I am sure he was dead before he even hit the pavement...All the pretence and the hidden shame of it. You see, because of his impoverished background, he was never considered good enough for my mother. That great British class divide. Even in his mid-seventies he was still trying hard to protect them from the savage eyes of this world. Those two upper-middle class, landed ladies had to be looked after and protected at all costs. That morning, as Alex succinctly put it, Sid hit the wall and just could not go on. The enormous pressure just told on him in the end.

(Jane wipes away some tears.)

Jane: I argued continuously with my father when he was alive. He seemed so old-fashioned to me. In truth, I sometimes felt ashamed of him. The way that he spoke. He was not a highly educated man. Yet now he is dead, I miss him terribly and only now begin to understand the horrendous pressure he must have been under those last few years…Poor darling! I hope that wherever he is now, he can find it in his heart to forgive me.

Leslie: Jane, you could not have done more. Do not torture yourself over it.

Marianne: Leslie is right, my dear. You are truly the dutiful, caring daughter. You accepted your role. What more could you have done?

Jane: Thank you both. I just cannot how hospitable, kind and considerate you two have been to complete and utter strangers like us. When Alex comes back, I think we should leave…You know, I do so want to believe. Want desperately to do the right thing, yet somehow, deep down inside, I just don't feel it. I feel disconnected all of the time…

Act 4

Scene: Inside the lounge in the flat upstairs in the house in Cornwall.

Alex: Can't you stop that bloody dog from barking! It's gone completely mad...Stop it for christsakes! That bitch is plain loco!

Jane: Sssh! She is upset, Alex.

Alex: Upset! You talk as if that bloody dog is a baby. A ferocious Doberman-Alsatian crossbred that has bitten its feral way through a five inch long metal key. Run amok throughout the downstairs house. Ripped fdown all the curtains in the front room lounge and ransacked Dorothy's bedroom for good measure. Blatantly done her business on the imitation Queen Anne chair, she's a holy terror!...Stop barking, you bitch! Shut up!...And you call her a baby! Who's crazy around here, I should like to know!

Jane: You are so very unkind. Trini leapt up to you and almost licked you to death when we arrived back this evening. I think she was doing her job and protecting the house. Guarding the homestead while we were away.

Alex: I'm surprised we didn't hear her barking down in Salcombe...What an infernal racket!

Jane: I reckon that someone or perhaps persons were trying to break into the house and Trini, good girl that she is, saw them off...That explains ho she managed to bit eclean through the metal key. She was so frantic, you see. She must have been determined fto frighten whoever was trying to break in. After all, it was all our fault, we should not have locked her in up here...

Alex: You think that yoiung builder who scowled at us this morning when qw set off and tried to hit us with his van door.

Jane: Yes, exactly.

Alex: You could well be right. God, I bet Trini gave him or them an almighty fright. I forgive her...Better?

Jane: She loves you.

Alex: Some love can make you quite uneasy, you know. Almost queasy, squeamish...Human nature is funny thiough, isn't it. You can get so all worked up and angry over something excessively annoying. Namely, the barking of a dog, a car engine revving continuously, unfriendly fireworks banging away non-stop throughout the night, then suddenly you find out a piece of information or make a discovery thatr the horrendous disturbance invading your mind space is being carried out by someone you know very well or are friends with, or maybe just an obvious explanation and, hey presto, the troublesome noise lessens. Your anger abates and finally disappears all together. Already, you see, I am warming to Trini's continual barking. I now understand that she is recounting the tale of bravery and I can definitely detect ancient rhythms and canine tones from across the dog centuries of human exposure.

Jane: You are a sarcastic bastard, Alex Croy…I'm so pleased we left Treetops Farm when we did. Mum was getting very tired. I liked the Bensons at first. Leslie Benson was most kind and considerate, but that Marianne Benson kept staring at you. She was actually devouring you with her eyes. No shame or subtlety. Right in front of her husband. Her two-faced conceit towards me. The cloying 'What it must be like to live with an artist. You are so lucky, Jane.' I nearly choked on my cucumber sandwich.

Alex: She was picking up on the anal heat between us.

Jane: Stop it!

Alex: Aarh, Trini has stopped barking at last. Do you want to go down and relieve poor Ben?

Jane: Susan will be here any minute now. Mum's half asleep. It's just to keep an eye on her in case she wakes up. It is so good of Susan, you know what can happen!

Alex: You mean Dorothy skipping naked through the Cornish village at one o'clock in the morning and Juggins here having to track her down and throw a blanket around her and lead her back home, dazed and confused.

Jane: Poor dear. She likes it when it's you. She always did prefer men.

Alex: That's no help when some sleep-headed, irate, Cornish local starts sneering at me. 'Can't you keep that old lady quiet! She should be locked up! Can't you control that old bitch!' and so on.

Jane: Please don't.

Alex: I'm sorry, Jane. I promise to make it up to you. Ever since I've known you, I've wanted to see you drip from every orifice.

Jane: That is absolutely disgusting.

Alex: No, it's not. It's very beautiful. True love in all its glory. No pretensions, no secrets, no distances, no hidden agendas, no walls of Jericho dividing bodies and minds.

Jane: I don't quite know if I am ready to surrender my last vestiges of dignity just yet. Please leave me something! I felt quite panic-stricken back at Treetops Farm when I looked up at you and my bottom...there, I've said it...started to quiver and shake. And you are right, that Marianne Benson did pick up on it. She sensed it.

Alex: Love is a summer sin.

Jane: What is wintertime then?

Alex: The season of madness.

Jane: Is that where my mother is then? In the season of wintertime madness?

Alex: Yes, I'm afraid so. Don't fret so. Dorothy has had a long life. It's just the natural order of things reasserting themselves. Mankind is so very conceited. It believes it can cheat death. That is why religions have been so successful over the many centuries.

Jane: Don't go there.

Alex: You are offering people the chance to live forever. How sweet is that. Cheat their own mortality. How could you fail to succeed with such a pitch. It is the ultimate salesman's dream. Help support me now, do as I say, and I will pray for you and when your ephemeral body decays and gives out, I will promise you now that you will have everlasting life. Great! Amen to that and where do I sign. Hey presto and away we go, but wait, the age-old dilemma **bewildering** mankind, and I'm being particularly generous to women here because I fully realise that they have carried the onerous load and sacrificed and struggled hard since the dawn of creation...Question? What vital proof do you possess? Answer...Well, you will just have to believe. Go beyond your human limitations. Really!...Believe in me and I can guarantee you immortality...I believe they call that a leap of faith...I wonder, Jane, how many deaths have resulted through fervent religious belief? Strange, isn't it. I am going to attain immortality through self-sacrifice, you do not believe the same as me and I am going to kill you and send you straight into nothingness forever. Amen to that and goodbye.

Jane: You have caused me to lose my religion. I never doubted til I met with you. Now I feel cut off, fractured in my soul and you have helped make me this way.

Alex: You credit me with far too much power, Jane. Hell, I am no shaman, no magician of the black arts, no spellbinding sorcerer. Christ, Jane, I can't even get my own books published and yet you treat me like I'm a long-lost descendant of John Dee down here on a visit. Never mind. Just remember this. The planet can be a very lonely place sometimes.

Jane: I do so hope that Susan gets here soon. Ben downstairs, dear angel, deserves a break. After all, just look at what he has had to put up with today. Why, when I was ten years old I was right at the centre of my own universe and everything was done for me automatically. Now, when I think back it is unbearable. Faces and thoughts just well up inside of me. I prayed and believed and felt so in control and just sailed straight on by everything with Mum, Dad and Auntie preparing every day for me. I was so aware and alive yet I now realise that a part of me was sleepwalking and that is where I miss my belief. It was my Guardian Angel, my saviour, my rock.

Alex: Simple answer. Stick the manhole cover back on the memories and we don't have to look at their faces.

Jane: Oh, that is so slickly trite! You are doing it again. Trying out lines on me again that you are going to use in your next novel. I do not want to be character cannon fodder for your material. Artists are such thieves, such filching magpies. They steal the moments out from other peoples' lives and use them for their own selfish ends. I will not be used in that way. You write about me and our lovemaking, don't you?

Alex: Your divine arsehole, Jane. Your divine arsehole.

Jane: I will sue you if you ever use me, do you hear. I do not wish to be exposed as a catamite before the world like that. How would you like it! Oh, I quite forgot, you are a totally shameless character, aren't you, and don't give a monkey's uncle!

Alex: There are a lot of monkeys about today, aren't there. I think I can hear Susan's car.

Jane: Don't you try and change the subject that easily. I am well versed in your tactics by now!

Alex: Well, it won't matter, will it, if I never ever get published. Who will ever see or read it.

Jane: That is not the point and you damn well know it. When you finish a book it will be put into the public domain. You will send it out to agents and publishers; my boys may stumble by accident across a copy of the manuscript. Mum might just pick it up by mistake.

Alex: Oh, come on, that is ridiculous and you know it. Anyway, you should be flattered. I bet that Marianne Benson would, just love and adore being based on a leading character in a novel. Fully reveal her innermost torments and secrets. Define the muse. Why worry yourself, the great unwashed public at large are never ever going to see or read it. Forget it.

Jane: You are forever going to keep bringing up Marianne Benson just to annoy and torment me, aren't you. I can see this continually happening. I am quite sure she would welcome the attention, though how she would feel about having a perpetually sore bottom...There I have gone and said it again...Like mine, all of the time, I can't rightly say.

Alex: I only have eyes for you, my dear. Think of me as the loving, reluctant freeloader, impassioned and imprisoned by you.

Jane: Stop it! Stop it! You do not really love me at all. I am just a swaying, succulent bottom to you. I have made all the running and effort in this relationship and all I ever get is rejection at every turn. Don't light that up please, you know what will happen! Do you have to smoke that stuff?

Alex: Whatever do you mean, Jane, dear? Would you buy a second-hand car from a dope-dealing salesman?

(Alex lights up his joint and puffs excessively.)

Jane: You selfish bastard! It will wake Mum up!

Alex: Well, look at it this way...*(puff)*...Sid lives on. His relentless effort to render every room in this house of Cornish gloom safe and smoke-free. A fire-breathing dragon would be carried out of here on a stretcher with fright. Exceeding even Sid's safety expectations.

(Suddenly, a smoke alarm is triggered and goes off loudly in the lounge room upstairs. This in turn activates all the other smoke alarms throughout the house.)

Jane: *(with her hands clamped over her ears and shouting)* See what you have gone and done, Alex Croy! You've set off all of the smoke alarms throughout the house! Are you happy now!

Alex: Eureka! It has stopped just like that!...Just for you I'll continually keep poking my head out of the window and blow smoke rings at the Cornish church spire. Maybe turn on a few seagulls and get them to tweet rather than screech. You happy now!

Jane: If you insist...Ben must have switched the alarm off. He is much cleverer than you give him credit for.

Alex: What do you mean! You know full well that I like the boy.

Jane: But you don't consider him especially bright, do you.

Alex: He possesses a heart of gold and that is more important than anything else. You're his mother, you should now that by now. But I suppose, as a mother, you want him to be a prodigal combination of Einstein, Gandhi and Napoleon all rolled into one.

Jane: Dad must have shown him inside the fuse box and all the different switches before he died.

Alex: Ben is an angelic listener with teal blue eyes.

Jane: Men are cleverer with mechanical things. It's their natural aptitude and element.

Alex: There you go again, splitting the human race back into two. Dividing us up, all fit to praise and to view. The biological necessity of being different. We are all born of mothers for the time being so we must be possessed of the same earthy rhythms.

Jane: For the time being?...Susan must have arrived back. I couldn't hear her car for the alarm noise.

Alex: Factory children are on the way so they say. I can envisage a future where the world will be governed by women. A society dominated by female scientists.

Jane: That is just your pure fantasy of being dominated by an all-powerful woman, a dominatrix, yet secretly you hate the very thought. You would lose your little boy status. You would no longer be able to charm your way out of one disaster after another.

Alex: Thank you for that sincere vote of confidence, Godless Sister. We shall see that Truth is the Daughter of all time. Isn't that a fact, Ben?

(Ben has been standing quietly for a while in the doorway of the upstairs

lounge flat.)

Jane: Oh, Ben, you are an angel, dear. So clever of you!

Ben: I only switched off the smoke alarm, Mum.

Jane: But you did it. Is your Grandmother alright? Did Susan...

Ben: Would I leave Gran on her own? I'll go downstairs and wait, Mum.

Jane: Yes, you do that, dear. Alex will give you a lift back home when we have finished.

Ben: Finished arguing.

Jane: We do not really argue, Ben. Well, we have, how shall I say, strong disagreements, but it is only our way of communicating. Ben, please be an absolute angel once again and go and wait downstairs as you said. Alex and I have some unfinished business to settle.

(Ben glides effortlessly out through the lounge flat door.)

Alex: You made that sound ominously serious.

Jane: Well, today has dredged up a lot of emotions and hidden thoughts for me. I thank you for taking us to Salcombe and for being so good with Mum. You know, seeing her there like that, totally unaware of her past life at Glebe Farm, Treetops now, of course...Well, that was odd in itself...I say myself projected into the future.

Alex: By the time you get there, hopefully there will have been huge medical advances. Scientists and doctors will have discovered a cure for Alzheimer's disease.

Jane: I think not.

Alex: Pessimist.

Jane: I was thinking not only of me, but the boys as well. It is all right for you to smile. What history do you have of Alzheimer's disease in your family tree?

Alex: Well, I shook the ancestral branches hard for three generations back and not one senile nutcase fell to earth.

Jane: You see...Why are you laughing at me in that way? That drug has made you stupid. Totally addled your brain. Stop it! Stop laughing at me, do you hear!

Alex: Anger is a dubious pleasure.

Jane: You bastard! After the day I have just been through. All my misgivings and fears raised up for my family. My boys...And you laugh at me like that! Why? What have I done to deserve this scorn? I have always believed in you, loved you, supported you. Could you please stop ridiculing me like that.

Alex: You are a total fraud, Jane. Alzheimer's disease a distinct possibility, more like selected amnesia, methinks...My family tree. Have you completely forgotten, Jane dear, has it entirely slipped your oh so genteel mind...You are adopted, Jane. You are not Dorothy's biological daughter. Auntie is not a blood relative of yours or am I missing some vital clue that's been kept from me...Oh, I get it. There was a weird third sister and you are her offspring, but nobody ever talked about it. They had her walled up somewhere in a hidden family vault. Just like Electra wailing her life away in demented torment and eternal damnation.

Jane: You are so very cruel and unkind. You have been all day long.

Alex: It takes more than one strong spliff to cloud my judgment. You are adopted, are you not, Godless Sister, or am I missing something here?

Jane: Oh, all right, if you so insist. Yes, I am adopted. Better? Yes, yes, yes!...I believe my mother was a secretary at one of the government ministries during the mid-fifties and had to give me up.

Alex: Did she have a history of Alzheimer's disease in her family tree?

Jane: I do not know anything else about her, as you bloody well know.

Alex: You could do a search.

Jane: I do not want to.

Alex: Afraid of what you might find?

Jane: Yes...Exactly.

Alex: Alright, Godless Sister. You want to belong so much you are even prepared to accept you adopted kin's diseases and wish to completely forget about your true origins...I do believe that

	Marianne Benson would have had a field day... *(Alex puts his left hand provocatively on his hip.)* Well, you don't have to worry, Jane, do you. Pout. Insincere smile. But, of course, my dear, you can never really know, can you. In its way that must be even worse, my dear, must it not... Poor Jane Leslie. Poor Jane!
Jane:	Stop it! Stop it! Stop it!...It's alright for you, Alex Croy, you have one of your great grandparents' wedding certificates. Battersea Town Hall, wasn't it? You can trace your family line back to the eighteen-sixties. Lucky you! Well, it's not that easy to accept when you are adopted. I never had any inkling until my Dad told me when I was thirteen years old. It came as a terrible shock to me. Understand, I have never fully gotten over it and I suppose until this day the lines had become blurred. You are always reminded in some little wee every day. Mum and Auntie were so wonderful with me. Neither of them had ever given birth to a child themselves and they treated me as their very own.
Alex:	And Sid?
Jane:	Oh, he took great pains on occasion after he'd told me, always well out of earshot of Mum and Auntie, of course, to make mention of it. By then I just knew I could never be biologically related to him.
Alex:	but it was because of him that you are here today. You look down on him and despise his poorhouse origins yet it was at his instigation that you were adopted in the first place.
Jane:	I don't feel that. He did what he was asked to do and for that I am grateful. The only time I've ever had any feelings or respect for him was after he'd died, when I fully realised just exactly what he had been hiding for the last two years of his life.
Alex:	So you could only warm to him in his death.
Jane:	If you must put it like that, yes... One of his farewell parting shots to me was that I would never get the better of you. He liked the idea of me being with you because he could see that for one in my life I had met my match and would not be able to get my own way all of the time.
Alex:	And have you always gotten your own way in life?
Jane:	Yes, up until now. Today, truly for the first time, I understand that everything around me is collapsing and what hurts most of all is your raw, naked violence towards me.
Alex:	Just a natural extension of our febrile, sexual indulgence. It is good to be out of control sometimes. You want everything

	organised, squared off and in its rightful place. It's like looking back at the past and seeing that everything was perfect when it never was, so today is always a crisis, that is the history of the human race. Even on a calm day, the ship is quietly leaking.
Jane:	And what do you feel, Alex Croy? Oh, I know you are only interested in the act of writing. All else is a distraction. Everything for your revolves around art and mystery. But does anything else really stir you and please don't answer my bottom. I would take it as a compliment, but I will not accept the carnal act of buggery as a spiritual driving force. Is there anything else or are you just an empty shell, a dead vessel with a sharp tongue and a good memory. A failed writer who can, how do you like to phrase it, sell the universe before lunchtime and spend the commission in the afternoon.
Alex:	Well, from the sound of your exasperated tone, I guess that makes me the shallow man expiring in a hollow screech. Right now I feel as if I am sat as the fourteenth guest on the duplication of the Last Supper. Outside of life. Excluded. About to be served up as a scapegoat. Hanged if I do and hanged if I don't!

(Jane turns quickly around and goes into the bathroom and shortly returns and puts a large tube of toothpaste on the upstairs lounge main table.)

Jane:	I was thinking of going into the garden centre at Lelant tomorrow. I do so want to buy some bougainvillea and was all set to ask you to venture into the church-walled garden to plant with me.
Alex:	Wrong season, Godless Sister. You being an April kind of a girl and all. You should know that. You don't plant in July, what are you thinking of?
Jane:	I just knew you would say that! You will not indulge me in my whims or idiosyncrasies one little bit, will you? Does the time of year matter? I do not really care if we buy up masses of bougainvillea and then within weeks they are all dead, blown away or pecked to death by your friends the screeching seagulls. I just want you to agree with me, and support me in an action no matter how small or inconsequential.
Alex:	Well, what about today and taking Dorothy to Salcombe and back? Wasn't that enough real life support for you?
Jane:	Oh, that was easy for you. That was real life drama. You are good at that. You like weddings, funerals, deadly violent scenes, catastrophes. Why? Don't answer. Because they are all potential material for your writing and you can play at being

this judgmental fourteenth person at the Last Supper, picking us all off one by one. No, do not interrupt. I want you to support me in a trivial act. Something unimportant. Indulge me if you like. Show solidarity in a minor matter. Give of yourself for once, but you are incapable…Funny, isn't it…I strive so hard to be careful and always do the right thing. That is what my life has been about up until now. Suddenly, money is no longer an urgent issue and instead of enjoyment my world starts crumbling around me and becoming merciless and unforgiving. Let me ask you a serious question, Alex Croy.

Alex: If you must.

Jane: When you go to clean your teeth, do you squeeze from the top of the tube of toothpaste or from the bottom?

Alex: Does it really matter?

Jane: It does to me and I have to know right now.

Alex: I don't see the point of this, but if you insist…I squeeze a tube of toothpaste from the bottom. Always have. I could lie and say that I don't really notice. I could prevaricate and say one day bottom, one day top, one day middle, one day I didn't clean my teeth at all, one day the toothbrush snapped in half, but I would be lying and you don't want me to lie to you, Jane, do you. Bottom…there you go…slowly…bottom…

Jane: I thought as much. The word bottom is no longer having its usual effect on me and I am pleased about that…You see, I always squeeze from the top of a tube of toothpaste and that means we are incompatible. We cannot live together.

Alex: But hang on, we use separate tubes of toothpaste. I'm Macleans to your Colgate. It doesn't make sense.

Jane: That is not the point, Alex Croy, and you bloody well know it! It is symbolic of our stuttering relationship.

Alex: But only last week you made me go to the bathroom, take off all of my clothes, lay naked with my back to the floor. You then stripped off all of your clothes, squatted down right over me and pissed all over my body in the ancient native Red Indian belief that the act of pissing on my naked flesh would bind me to you forever!

Jane: Well, I was wrong, wasn't I. That just goes to show you how desperate you have made me!

Alex: Okay then, I will go and drive Ben back home. Come back and pack my things. I will leave tomorrow morning if you really want me to.

Jane: Thank you.

Lightning Source UK Ltd.
Milton Keynes UK
UKHW021102080422
401284UK00011B/330